For Diana
—KD

For Anya and her two big sisters!
—JM

 little bee books

A division of Bonnier Publishing
853 Broadway, New York, New York 10003
Text copyright ©2016 by Kristy Dempsey
Illustrations copyright © 2016 by Jane Massey
Manufactured in China LEO 0816
First Edition 10 9 8 7 6 5 4 3 2 1
ISBN 978-1-4998-0236-8

littlebeebooks.com
bonnierpublishing.com

Library of Congress Cataloging-in-Publication Data:
Names: Dempsey, Kristy, author. | Massey, Jane, 1967- illustrator.
Title: Ten little toes, two small feet / by Kristy Dempsey ; illustrated by Jane Massey.
Description: NewYork : Little Bee Books, [2016]
Summary: Toddlers crawl, play, and walk as they help the reader learn to count to ten.
Identifiers: LCCN 2015049654 | ISBN 9781499802368 (hardback)
Subjects: | CYAC: Stories in rhyme. | Toes—Fiction. | Toddlers—Fiction. | Counting. | BISAC: JUVENILE FICTION / Concepts /
Counting & Numbers. | JUVENILE FICTION / Family / New Baby. | JUVENILE FICTION / Family / Parents.
Classification: LCC PZ8.3.D4315 Tet 2016 | DDC [E]—dc23
LC record available at https://lccn.loc.gov/2015049654

Ten Little Toes, Two Small Feet

by Kristy Dempsey illustrated by Jane Massey

 little bee books

Two small feet, toe by toe.

Ten little toes all in a row!

Ten little toes on two small feet.

These ten toes are ten times sweet.

Ten little toes up in the air.

Five toes here and five toes there.

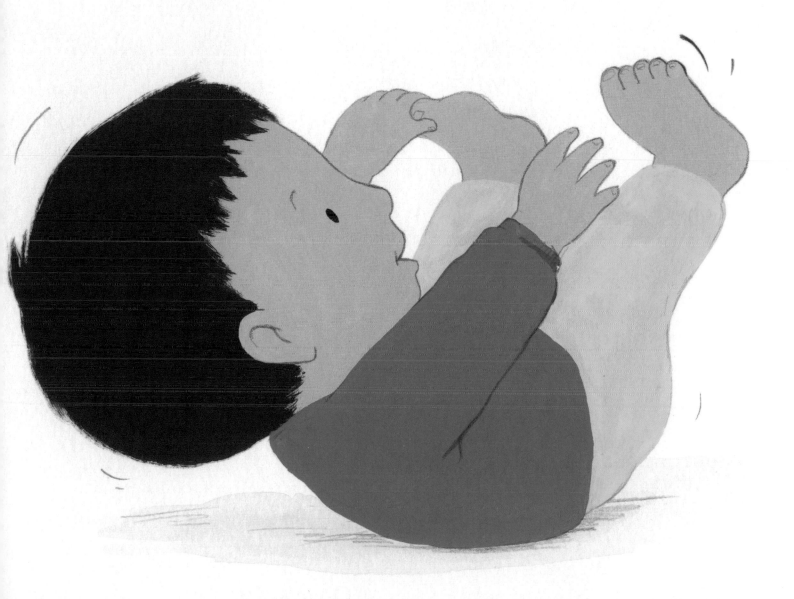

Ten toes curl, ten toes tap.

Ten toes peek out from a nap.

Ten toes trail across the floor,

crawling through the backyard door.

Ten toes tickle, ten toes wriggle.

Ten toes squish and ten toes wiggle.

Ten toes make a muddy path.

These ten toes
should take a bath!

Ten toes splash, ten toes splatter.

Ten clean toes, pitter-patter.

Ten toes step, wibble-wobble.

Ten toes walking! Baby-bobble.

Baby bumps, baby cries.

Kiss ten toes and
dry your eyes.

Two feet touch the floor and then . . .

Ten little toes are off again!